YOU'VE GOT THIS!

An Hachette UK Company
www.hachette.co.uk

Vie Books, an imprint of Summersdale Publishers Ltd
Part of Octopus Publishing Group Limited
Carmelite House
50 Victoria Embankment
LONDON
EC4Y 0DZ
UK

www.summersdale.com

Printed and bound in China

ISBN: 978-1-78685-801-6

Substantial discounts on bulk quantities of Summersdale books are available to corporations, professional associations and other organizations. For details contact general enquiries: telephone: +44 (0) 1243 771107 or email: enquiries@summersdale.com.

Neither the author nor the publisher can be held responsible for any loss or claim arising out of the use, or misuse, of the suggestions made herein. None of the views or suggestions in this book is intended to replace medical opinion from a doctor. If you have any concerns about your health, please seek professional advice.

YOU'VE GOT THIS!

Release Your Inner Power and Be Awesomely You

POPPY O'NEILL

vie

CONTENTS

FOREWORD

Today's teenagers seem to have an unending array of stressors, comparisons and concerns that negatively impact their sense of self. These include peer pressure, the stress of exams and assessments, the relentless onslaught of social media, together with the hormonal and body changes that occur as they transition through puberty. All of these were having a damaging effect on young people's mental health long before the current the time of Covid, which has since had the effect of throwing proverbial petrol onto the pre-existing mental health bonfire.

Poppy O'Neill's latest book, *You've Got This!* is a comprehensive resource to help young people enhance and develop their self-esteem. The outline of the book is immediately accessible and inviting, steering clear of heady explanations or wordy discussions so often found in resources of this kind. Poppy takes readers through a simple yet structured approach to explaining self-esteem, what it is and the reasons why young people may suffer from a lack of it.

She then explores self-esteem boosters, such as mindfulness, the importance of gratitude and journaling, before going on to consider the important topic of how to tackle negative self-talk. Recognizing that no one strategy is going to work for every young person, Poppy offers a wide range of strategies designed to help and boost self-esteem, ranging from recognizing "thoughts aren't facts" to "how to respond to negative self-talk". The book completes with chapters on self-care and the importance of friendships, which includes a section on the impact that social media can play in the life of a teenager.

I would highly recommend this book which can be used as a stand-alone resource or as a guide to help supplement any pre-existing therapy.

Graham Kennedy MA, UKCP Reg
Integrative Child & Adolescent Psychotherapist
Attachment and Trauma Consultant

April 2021

INTRODUCTION

Welcome to *You've Got This!*, a guide to building up your self-esteem and keeping it strong. When you have high self-esteem, you feel good about yourself and your capabilities. Building a strong sense of self will see you through tough times and challenges.

In your teenage years, your brain changes and grows at an incredible rate. This means you're able to learn new skills and information, and you have so much creative potential, but you're also more susceptible to pressure and negative messages from others and the world around you. Peer pressure, exam stress, puberty, social media and a growing awareness of the world around you can all make you feel like you're never quite good enough or never doing enough and that everyone else seems to be breezing through life... It's exhausting!

With a mix of activities, ideas and proven techniques used by therapists, like cognitive behavioural therapy (CBT) and mindfulness, this book will help you shift how you think about yourself, how you see others and how you feel about your place in the world.

IT'S OK NOT TO FEEL OK

Everyone else makes it look so easy. Relationships, school, how they look... Does it sometimes feel like you're the only one struggling?

The good news is, you're not alone. Other people are not noticing your imperfections – they are thinking about their own imperfections, the ones you don't see because you're worrying about your own.

It's OK to struggle. It's OK to need help. It's OK to need reassurance or support or a damn good cry. You are just as deserving of these things as anybody else in the world. You are not a burden; you are a human being, and you are loved. There are people in your life who care about you and want to know what it's like to be you. They want to know when it's hard, when you're feeling stuck or hopeless or heartbroken.

So take a deep breath and know that you are allowed to be exactly as you are right now. You don't have to have it all figured out.

WHAT THIS BOOK WILL DO FOR YOU

This book will help you understand how self-esteem works, as well as show you how to improve yours and keep it high – even during tough times.

The more you learn about yourself, the more in control of your thoughts and feelings you'll be.

So if you're sick of feeling less than everyone else, and you're ready to stop listening to those annoying negative thoughts, you've come to the right place.

A strong, confident I've-got-this attitude is already inside you, and this book will help you to uncover it. So read on and remember: you've got this!

HOW TO USE THIS BOOK

This book is for you if...

★ **You go along with the crowd.**

★ **You hide things about yourself.**

★ **You compare yourself to other people.**

★ **You need likes and compliments to feel good.**

★ **You feel like you're not good enough.**

★ **You feel like you need to be perfect.**

★ **You worry about how you look.**

If this sounds like you sometimes, or *all* the time, this book is here to help. How you feel about yourself can change, and you have the power to change it for the better.

Inside these pages you'll find all sorts of ideas for building up your self-esteem, so you can feel more confident and comfortable being you.

This book is about you, so take it at your own pace. Some of the things inside will feel useful and others not so much, and it's OK to go with what feels right for you.

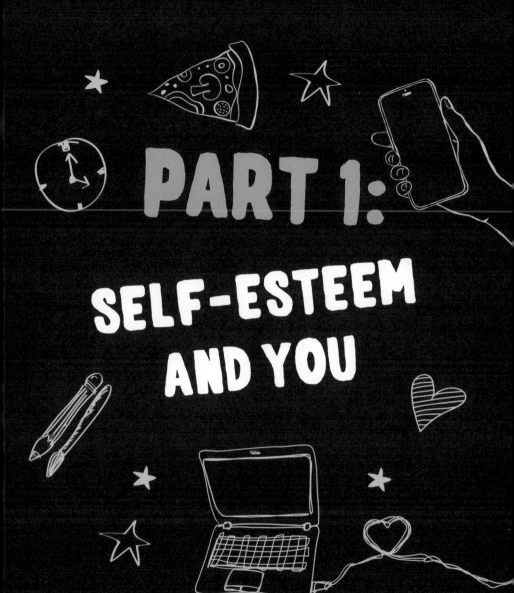

PART 1:

SELF-ESTEEM AND YOU

HOW DO YOU FEEL ABOUT YOURSELF?

Self-esteem
noun

Confidence in one's own worth
or abilities; self-respect.

Self-esteem is all about how you feel about yourself. It can be high
(like when you feel super-confident and really proud of yourself) or
low (such as when you feel like you've failed and you're the worst
person in the entire universe), or somewhere in between.

Humans are complicated, so self-esteem develops differently for
everyone. Lots of things can influence your self-esteem (more on that
later), and it can go up and down, depending on what you're doing,
who you're with or what's going on in your body.

I MATTER.

I MATTER EQUALLY.

NOT "IF ONLY".

NOT "AS LONG AS".

I MATTER EQUALLY.

FULL STOP.

Chimamanda Ngozi Adichie

ALL ABOUT ME

Getting to know yourself is a really important part of building healthy self-esteem. The better you know yourself, the more in touch you are with what's important to you, as well as what you like and dislike – so it's easier to stand up for yourself. Here are some prompts to get you thinking. Jot down your answers in the spaces below or grab an extra piece of paper if you feel inspired to write more!

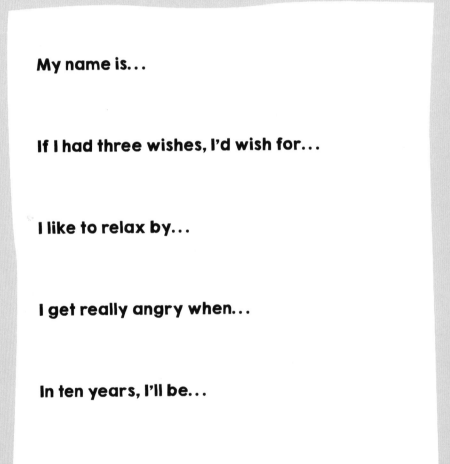

My name is...

If I had three wishes, I'd wish for...

I like to relax by...

I get really angry when...

In ten years, I'll be...

I can't live without...

I'm really good at...

My favourite song is...

I've always wanted to visit...

If I could ask my great-great-great-great-great-grandparents a question, I'd ask...

One thing I find really difficult is...

The nicest thing anyone's ever said to me is...

WHAT HIGH SELF-ESTEEM FEELS LIKE

Saying "no" to things you don't want to do	Feeling OK with making mistakes	Feeling energetic	Feeling hopeful for the future
Believing in yourself	Respecting others' differences	Encouraging others	Celebrating your achievements
Being a good winner and a good loser	Feeling comfortable spending time alone	Feeling OK with being single	Standing up for yourself
Knowing that you're a good person	Speaking your mind	Being OK with disagreement	Looking after your body

WHAT LOW SELF-ESTEEM FEELS LIKE

Needing to be perfect	Needing to agree with others	Going along with the crowd	Putting yourself down
Feeling jealous	Thinking you are not as good as everyone else	Needing compliments or likes to feel OK	Negative thinking
Disrespecting other people	Not looking after your body	Spending time with people who are unkind to you	Worrying about how you look
Speaking unkindly to other people	Needing other people to agree with you	Keeping quiet in order to fit in	Feeling bad about your achievements

IF WE TREATED OURSELVES THE WAY WE TREATED OUR BEST FRIEND, CAN YOU IMAGINE HOW MUCH BETTER OFF WE'D BE?

Meghan, Duchess of Sussex

HOW DO YOU FEEL RIGHT NOW?

Take some time to think about how you feel right at this moment by considering the statements below.

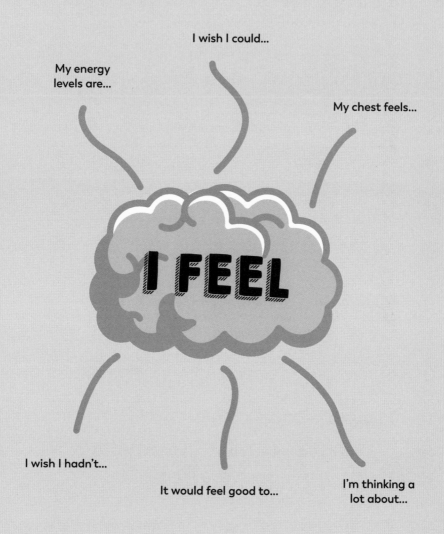

I wish I could...

My energy levels are...

My chest feels...

I FEEL

I wish I hadn't...

It would feel good to...

I'm thinking a lot about...

THE SELF-ESTEEM QUIZ

Take this quiz to see how high or low your self-esteem is right now. Circle the answer that sounds most like you... Results are on the next page.

I'm good at...

    a)   Plenty of things

    b)   Nothing, really

    c)   One or two things

When I compare myself to others, I feel...

    a)   Like I'm good and so are they

    b)   Worse than them

    c)   Better than them

Perfection is...

    a)   Not a real thing!

    b)   The need to be perfect or I won't be liked

    c)   Something I never quite achieve

If I make a mistake, I...

    a)   Try to put it right

    b)   Look for someone else to blame

    c)   Feel super-guilty

My friends...

a)   Are fun, kind and great to talk to

b)   Put me down, but at least they talk to me

c)   Are OK, I guess

When I do well...

a)   I feel proud of myself

b)   I think I should have done better

c)   I feel embarrassed to talk about it

Saying "no" is...

a)   Sometimes tricky, but I do it anyway

b)   Unkind

c)   Something I try to avoid

Mostly As: you have high self-esteem! You have heaps of self-respect, and you know how to treat yourself and others well. This book will help you strengthen it even more, as well as recognize the signs of low self-esteem in others.

Mostly Bs: your self-esteem is pretty low. You tend to put yourself last, and you worry about what other people think of you – even if they treat you badly. You could do with a big self-esteem boost. Your feelings matter.

Mostly Cs: you could do with working on your self-esteem. You know how to give yourself a boost when you're feeling down, which is great. Strengthening your self-esteem will help you feel good about yourself, whatever happens.

**Turn the page to learn more about growing
your self-esteem – you can do this!**

WHAT AFFECTS YOUR SELF-ESTEEM?

When you're a teen, lots of things can knock your self-esteem. Changes in your body and brain make this a particularly vulnerable time for how you feel about yourself. Here are just a few of the big influences in your life that can affect self-esteem during your teenage years:

* Friendships
* Relationships
* Puberty
* Your parents
* Social media

* Celebrities
* Past experiences
* Teachers
* Exams
* Schoolwork

Building healthy self-esteem means that your sense of who you are comes from within. Whether you fit in, what people think and things that happen to you might knock your self-confidence, but with healthy self-esteem you'll be more resilient and able to get back to feeling good about yourself quickly.

WHAT PEOPLE THINK OF ME IS NONE OF MY BUSINESS.

Tracee Ellis Ross

HOW LOW SELF-ESTEEM CAN AFFECT YOUR LIFE

I don't feel confident speaking up when I have a different opinion to the rest of my friendship group.

I participated in online bullying because I knew it would get likes.

I never sent off my article to the writing competition because I didn't think it would be good enough.

For way too long, I stayed with a boyfriend who put me down and cheated on me.

I used to love painting, but I'd get so upset if I made a mistake so I don't bother any more.

I dropped out of the football team because I was worried about how my legs looked in shorts.

HOW CAN YOU GO FROM LOW TO HIGH SELF-ESTEEM?

Building self-esteem can feel really strange. If you've never considered it before, the way you think and feel about yourself probably just seems like "the truth", and you assume that's how everyone else thinks about you, too.

Everyone is different, so where you start is personal to you. Working towards higher self-esteem involves deeply and carefully considering your thoughts and actions, asking yourself questions, and slowly changing the way you see yourself.

Sure, there are ways to get a quick self-esteem boost (like posting a selfie online or donating to charity), as well as stuff that will knock your self-esteem temporarily (like tripping over in public or failing a test), but we tend to come back to roughly the same level once we've moved on from these boosts and knocks.

By raising your self-esteem, you'll be able to come back to feeling good about yourself, whatever happens.

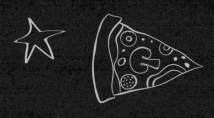

PART 2:

SELF-ESTEEM
BOOSTERS

NEED A BOOST?

Sometimes we all need a push in the right direction to overcome fear and act with confidence. Boosts like these are really useful in building self-esteem, because they help to get you out of your comfort zone, break cycles of negative thinking and create new experiences... all of which goes towards raising your self-esteem levels.

Building strong self-esteem takes more than temporary boosts, but we'll get to that later. In this section you'll find quick ways to supercharge your confidence.

TRY MEDITATION

Meditation is a great way to start getting to know your mind and emotions. It might feel weird or difficult at first, but the more you do it, the easier it gets. Meditation literally changes the structure of your brain – helping you to feel less stressed and more able to manage your emotions, as well as improving your relationships with others.

You can meditate anywhere, but a comfy chair in a quiet room is a good place to try it out. Here's how to get started:

★ **Set a timer for three minutes or choose a relaxing song to listen to (when you get to the end of the tune, you'll know you can finish meditating).**

★ **Sit comfortably.**

★ **Close your eyes.**

★ **Think about your breathing: how each breath in feels, and then how each breath out feels. Don't hold your breath in between – just try to breathe slowly in through your nose, then out through your nose. Listen to the sound of your breath.**

★ **If other thoughts come into your mind, don't worry – that's normal. Just let them float out again.**

★ **When the timer goes or the music ends, open your eyes slowly.**

The idea is that if you focus on the sound and feeling of your breath, your brain doesn't have time to think about other stuff. This makes meditation a great thing to do if you're struggling with negative thoughts or difficult feelings.

How did meditating make you feel? Circle the feelings you can relate to:

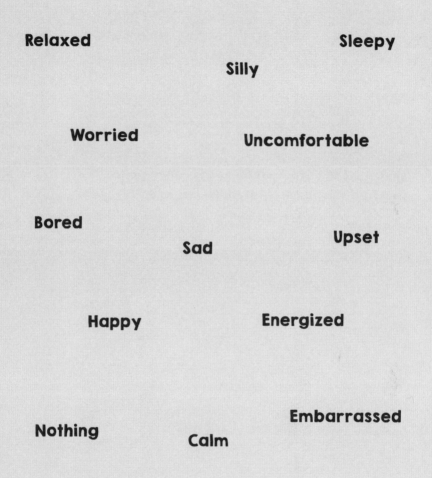

Relaxed   Sleepy

                        Silly

       Worried   Uncomfortable

Bored
                                              Upset
                 Sad

       Happy   Energized

                                     Embarrassed
Nothing
                        Calm

However meditating made you feel, it's OK. It can be super-weird being alone with your thoughts all of a sudden. Like anything, it takes practice to get comfy meditating. Try it again for three minutes every few days, and see if it starts to feel easier.

WHAT MAKES YOU FEEL GOOD (AND HOW CAN YOU DO MORE OF IT)?

Everyone has different things that make them feel good – and they help you build self-esteem. Write a list below, using these questions to get you started...

What makes you feel amazing? When do you feel most like yourself? When do you laugh most? When do you feel really peaceful?

How could you do *more* of these things? Can you do one of them every day?

WHAT MAKES YOU FEEL BAD?

There are some places and people that just seem to make us feel bad about ourselves. It might be a teacher who's quite negative, or a shop where the clothes always make you feel like there's something wrong

Can you think of two or three situations that are sure to knock your self-esteem?

Could you change your routine or habits so you can spend less time doing these things? If not, are there changes you could make that would help you to feel better about yourself? For example, "I can choose to only visit shops that sell clothes I feel good wearing."

LISTEN TO YOUR THOUGHTS

What's on your mind at this moment? Pause to take notice of the thoughts in your head. You might find lots of random ideas, or something in particular taking up your headspace, like a trip you're looking forward to or a disagreement with a friend. Try writing your thoughts here, on some scrap paper or in a notebook:

Sometimes just jotting something down can make you feel better. It's almost like you're moving the thoughts out of your head and onto the paper. If you're worried that what you write is weird or uninteresting, remember that you don't need to show anyone: it's just for you! Once you're done, you can keep what you've written, show it to someone (only if you want to), or screw it up and throw it away.

If writing out your thoughts feels good, you might like to start keeping a journal. You can write whatever you feel like in it, as often as you want. It doesn't need to be anything fancy – just a basic notebook works perfectly.

Here's a brilliant way of using a journal to boost your self-esteem:

Draw a line down the centre of the page, like this:

On this side, write your negative thoughts. Don't hold back.	And on this side, write answers to those negative thoughts, as if talking to your best friend.

Many studies have found that writing down your thoughts helps to reduce depression, stress and anxiety. It works because putting pen to paper helps you to process and organize them in a way that's difficult to achieve while they're stuck in your mind.

MAKE AN "I'VE GOT THIS" JAR

What is it? A jar full of little self-esteem boosts that you can dip into whenever you're feeling down about yourself. The notes you keep in the jar will remind you of all the good things in your life and the reasons why you're amazing.

You will need:
paper, scissors and an empty jar.

How to make it:
Cut your paper into lots of squares, roughly 5 cm x 5 cm (2 in. x 2 in.).

On each square, write something that makes you feel good – a memory, an achievement, a compliment, something you love to do, something you're looking forward to, a line from a show that always cracks you up... whatever you can think of!

Our day at the beach

"You're the best and most hilarious friend in the universe."
– Amelia

Coming second in the poetry competition

I can do hard things

Now fold or roll each square and put it in the jar.

Whenever you feel down, pick a random square from the jar and it will give you a little self-esteem boost.

WHAT IS MINDFULNESS AND WHY SHOULD I TRY IT?

Mindfulness is a concept that originated in Buddhist philosophy. Researchers have looked into its benefits, and have found that it has a remarkable effect on the mind and emotions, reducing anxiety, combatting stress and increasing self-esteem. It's basically about giving all your attention to what is happening right at this moment... but it's much cooler than that. Mindfulness is a way to train your brain to think differently.

You know how sometimes you can do dumb things when you're really angry, upset or excited? That's because when you feel a big emotion, your limbic system (the part of your brain responsible for emotions) takes over and your cortex (the part of your brain that does the rational thinking) takes a back seat, so you're *feeling* rather than *thinking about* your actions.

Practising mindfulness helps you to navigate your feelings more effectively, by allowing you to pause between feeling and doing. When you use mindfulness, you learn to feel safe with your emotions, even when they're really difficult. This, in turn, makes you more resilient and less likely to do something you'll later regret.

HOW TO BE MINDFUL

You can do almost anything mindfully. You can type mindfully, walk mindfully, stare out of the window mindfully, take a shower mindfully... You get the picture.

Here's how to eat mindfully:

Take a snack - let's say it's a cookie. Give your full attention to the cookie. The cookie is your whole universe for the next minute.

Before you even take a bite, feel the weight of the cookie in your hand. Run your finger along its edges. Sniff the cookie.

Take a bite of the cookie - how does it feel on your lips? Notice the different tastes and textures you can detect. Chew slowly, and feel how the tastes and textures change in your mouth. Keep going like this until the cookie is all gone.

Now you've eaten a cookie mindfully, you can do a minute of mindfulness any time, anywhere! All you need to do is slow down and appreciate every small detail of any experience.

FEEL-GOOD AFFIRMATIONS

An affirmation is a positive statement that helps you challenge negative thoughts, and the more you repeat it, the more you believe it. Different affirmations work for different people, so try a few out and see which ones feel good to you:

I AM STRONG.

MY BODY IS PRECIOUS.

I CAN DO HARD THINGS.

I BELIEVE IN MYSELF.

I DESERVE KINDNESS.

I AM GRATEFUL TO BE ME.

MY FEELINGS MATTER.

I AM LOVED.

I AM SUCCESSFUL.

I AM SAFE.

I CAN SAY "no".

I AM OK.

I CAN DO THIS.

I AM BEAUTIFUL.

I AM POWERFUL.

I LIKE WHO I AM.

I CAN DO GREAT THINGS.

I AM A SPECIAL PERSON.

I AM ENOUGH.

MY VOICE MATTERS.

I DESERVE TO BE TREATED WELL.

I RESPECT MYSELF.

Once you've picked an affirmation or two that feel good to you, why not write them on Post-its and put them somewhere you'll see them every day, like a mirror or inside your locker at school. Or turn to page 70 and make an affirmation poster.

QUICK SELF-ESTEEM BOOSTERS

Go outside – science has found that nature boosts mental health in many ways: vitamin D from sunlight, reconnecting with our senses and gentle exercise are just some of them.

Smile – even if you don't feel like it. The act of smiling releases feel-good brain chemicals called endorphins that trick your brain so you feel a bit better instantly.

Take a deep breath – increasing the oxygen in your body is a simple way to boost your confidence and energy levels, while reducing stress and anxiety. Each time you breathe out, your heart rate slows, coming into sync with your breathing.

Relax your shoulders and unclench your jaw – sometimes we don't realize that we're holding our bodies in a really tense way. Take a moment to notice your shoulders and your jaw – could you relax them a little more?

Tidy up – whether it's one shelf or your entire bedroom, tidying up helps to calm anxiety and raise self-esteem. Improving the world around you (even just a little bit) makes you feel good inside.

Get creative – drawing, painting, dancing, skating... How do you like to get creative? However you do it, being free to make or do something just for fun is a great self-esteem booster, as it allows your mind to relax and have fun.

Journal – writing down your thoughts and feelings boosts self-esteem by giving you space to put yourself first, without worrying about the judgement of other people.

Exercise – moving your body is a great way to feel better about yourself. Exercise brings your focus away from your thoughts and into your body, making it an excellent mindful activity.

Listen to music – music can change your mood quickly! What songs make you feel epic? Listen to those when you feel down on yourself. You could even make a self-esteem-boosting playlist.

YOU ARE UNIQUE

What makes you different is what makes you great. Think about it: do you love your close friends because of their identical hairstyles or their flawless skin? No! It's their quirks, their weirdness, their random qualities that set them apart from others.

It's exactly the same with you. You are a unique blend of personality, characteristics, experiences, appearance, strengths and weaknesses. No one can replace you because no one is quite like you.

Sure, being yourself will mean that you don't get along with everyone, and that's completely fine. Good, even. Imagine how exhausting it would be if everyone wanted to be your bestie!

When you let your real self shine, those who fit with you will find you. And others will find friends who fit with them. There's no need to worry that anyone else is better than you or try to build yourself up by thinking that you are better than anyone else. We're all simply different, and that's awesome.

THERE'S A WHOLE CATEGORY OF PEOPLE WHO MISS OUT BY NOT ALLOWING THEMSELVES TO BE WEIRD ENOUGH.

Alain de Botton

GET TALKING

Talking about your feelings – do you find it easy, cringeworthy... a bit frightening?

Chances are, if your self-esteem is quite low right now, talking about your feelings isn't easy at all. When you don't feel good about yourself, your mind might trick you into believing that your feelings don't matter or that no one wants to listen to them.

It's true that not everyone will react kindly when you talk about your feelings. It's a good idea to choose someone you trust – a parent, carer, teacher, friend or relative that you feel comfortable with and who you know is kind.

Talking about your feelings is one of the most powerful and brave things you can do. When we talk about our feelings with someone who's a good listener, our worries get smaller, and difficult emotions get easier.

Here are a few ways you could start a conversation about feelings and mental health:

Can I just vent to you for a minute, please?

I find this quite hard – can I tell you something?

I've noticed I'm feeling different lately...

**I read something that's really made me think
– can I share it with you?**

There's something bugging me – is it a good time to talk?

This feels really awkward, but I think I need your help.

Could you listen to me for a bit?

Can I talk to you about something personal?

WHO CAN I TALK TO?

Write down the person (or people) in your life you can talk to about your feelings. What makes each one a good listener?

If you don't have anyone that you feel OK talking to, check the resources on page 140 – you're not alone and there is help available.

GRATITUDE JOURNALING

Thinking up things you're grateful for helps you to focus on the positives. Some days it can be a challenge, and when you can find something good about even the most rubbish day, that's a real boost!

Quick – think of three things you're grateful for:

1.

2.

3.

If you get stuck, try thinking of something you have, something that happened and something about you.

Making a gratitude list is a great habit to practise before you go to sleep. You could write your list in your journal or a notebook, or just think of three good things before you close your eyes.

WE NEED TO DO A BETTER JOB OF PUTTING OURSELVES HIGHER ON OUR OWN "TO-DO" LIST.

Michelle Obama

YOU ARE OK AS YOU ARE

There's a lot in this book about how to raise your self-esteem, and it can sometimes feel like self-esteem is something you're failing at! So it's important you know that it's OK to have low self-esteem. It's OK to feel sad, or embarrassed, or angry, or jealous... Whatever you are feeling at any moment is OK.

The aim is not to have perfect self-esteem. That is just as impossible as having perfect skin. A person with flawless skin would probably be a robot. And the same goes for anyone with 100 per cent bulletproof self-esteem: probably a robot.

Sometimes we do mess up, and we all have flaws. The aim is to shift the way you think about yourself, so that your self-talk is kinder and more patient. Then when you mess up, your thoughts will bring you a bit of comfort rather than yelling at you.

MY SELF-ESTEEM FIRST-AID KIT

In this section we've discovered some of the ways you can boost your self-esteem quickly. Now it's time to put together a first-aid kit for when you're feeling down and need some fast feel-good energy.

On this page, write the things that give you a real boost – you can come back to it any time you need.

I can talk to...

An idea that helps me...
(E.g. don't compare yourself to others)

An activity that helps me...
(E.g. gratitude journaling)

Remember that...
(E.g. I am OK as I am)

A movie that makes me feel good...

A song that fills me with confidence...

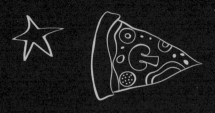

PART 3:

HOW TO TACKLE NEGATIVE SELF-TALK

WHAT IS SELF-TALK?

Self-talk is the way we talk to ourselves. Usually not out loud, but in our minds. Everyone has self-talk. It's the voice that you hear when you make a mistake or when you look in the mirror. If you have low self-esteem, that voice is probably a bit of a jerk.

The good news is, that voice isn't the truth, and it's certainly not the real you. With hard work and dedication, you can change your self-talk, making it more like a best friend than a bully.

GET TO KNOW YOUR SELF-TALK

Take a moment to sit quietly by yourself and listen to your thoughts. Can you hear that inner voice? Is it being a total jerk about anything right now?

Perhaps you failed a test at school or you worry about how you look. What does that inner voice have to say? If you feel OK to, you can write it here:

(Now you can do what you like with what you've just written. Keep it, scribble it out, write something kinder in bold letters...)

You can spot negative self-talk every time by the way it's always repeating itself. It will use the same words or tell you the same story about yourself.

Can you sketch what this unkind inner voice would look like if it were a person or creature? Can you think of a name for it? (How about Self-Talk Slimeball or Negative Noodle from Outer Space?)

Next time you hear that negative self-talk voice in your head, you can roll your eyes, knowing it's just the Negative Noodle going blah, blah, blah.

THOUGHTS AREN'T FACTS

It's easy to believe that everything we think about ourselves and the world around us is true. Our thoughts are heavily influenced by our feelings, so if you feel down about yourself, your thoughts are going to reflect that and you might also project your feelings onto other people.

Projection: when you see the world through your feelings. For example, if you feel like a bad person and assume other people think that, too, without any evidence that they do.

Thoughts are just thoughts... They aren't facts. You can think anything you choose – impossible thoughts, boring thoughts, kind thoughts, anxious thoughts – but thinking something doesn't make it true. For example, perhaps you're worrying that it'll rain on your birthday. Thinking those thoughts won't change the weather, but it might change your mood.

If you get stuck in negative thinking, it's OK... everyone does sometimes. The trick is not to try to stop these thoughts, but to simply take less notice of them.

THOUGHTS AND FACTS QUIZ

When you spot negative thoughts starting to fill up your mind, try asking yourself these questions:

★ **Am I being fair to myself? (E.g. it's not fair to think I should be perfect.)**

★ **Is it helpful to me to think this? (E.g. it's not helpful to think I am going to fail before I've even tried.)**

★ **Is it likely to be true? (E.g. it's not likely that my friends all secretly find me annoying.)**

★ **Is it based on facts? (E.g. "I'm ugly" is not a fact.)**

★ **What facts prove this thought wrong? (E.g. I have learned a new skill before and now I have mastered it.)**

★ **Would I say this to my best friend? (If not, why are you saying it to yourself?!)**

You could think through these questions, or write the answers out in a journal or notebook.

TALK TO YOURSELF LIKE YOU WOULD TO SOMEONE YOU LOVE.

Brené Brown

WHAT'S THE WORST THAT COULD HAPPEN... AND THE BEST?

As we know, thoughts aren't facts, so you're free to try out different ones any time. Whenever you're feeling down about yourself or negative about something, try this exercise.

What's the worst that could happen?

This might be scary to think about... but research shows that it helps to express your insecurities and anxieties, whether in a journal, speaking to someone you trust or just admitting them to yourself. Try saying or writing: "I'm really worried that _____ will happen."

And what's the best that could happen?

Start small if this is tricky; for example, "This could be OK..." Then see if you can imagine something even better, like: "This could go really well."

Take some time to picture a positive outcome. Close your eyes and visualize yourself doing well; imagine how that would feel, and what it would look like. Add as much detail as you can, so it feels really real.

> Positive thoughts won't change your self-esteem straight away, but if you get in the habit of thinking more positively, you'll begin to believe in yourself a little more each time, and your self-esteem will start to grow.

HOW PAST EXPERIENCES CAN AFFECT YOUR SELF-ESTEEM

Your brain's main job is to keep you safe. It remembers almost everything that happens to you and how it makes you feel. So if you once burned your hand on a hot oven, your brain will make sure you're extra-careful around ovens.

What's that got to do with self-esteem?

Feeling embarrassed or rejected is just as important to our brains as physical pain like a burn. So if you've had a bad experience in the past, your brain will make sure you're aware of things that remind it of that. It will trick you into thinking that it's not worth trying again when something went wrong or felt uncomfortable before.

Low self-esteem is your brain's way of trying to keep you safe from things that happened in the past... which doesn't make much sense when you think about it (unless you happen to have a time machine).

HOW TO RESPOND TO NEGATIVE SELF-TALK

It's OK to have negative thoughts: if you try to push them away or pretend they don't happen, they'll just pop back up later.

The trick is to learn all you can about how your mind works, so that you will be able to understand why a particular thought is visiting you at a particular time.

For example, if you're thinking negatively about your weight, it could be because you just saw a weight-loss advert on the internet or you overheard someone else talking judgementally about their body. We all exist in a world full of messages, some of which our minds absorb and some they don't.

You can accept your thoughts without believing they are true.

HOW YOUR THOUGHTS ARE HOLDING YOU BACK

Low self-esteem can develop when the brain responds to strong negative feelings with what psychologists call "thinking errors". These are ways of thinking about yourself and the world around you that make negative thoughts and emotions feel true.

Here are the most common thinking errors, and how to spot them:

All-or-nothing thinking: if this isn't perfect, I've failed completely.

Over-generalizing: if one thing goes wrong, everything will go wrong.

Focusing on the negative: if one thing goes wrong, that's the only thing I can think about – despite other things going right.

Fortune-telling: I know I'll fail.

Mind-reading: I know everyone will think badly of me.

Catastrophizing: one mistake will ruin everything.

Magnified thinking: the things
I dislike about myself are the
most important things about
me. The things I like about
myself aren't important.

Negative comparison:
my friend is better
than me in every way.

Unrealistic
expectations:
I should be perfect
at everything.

Putting yourself
down: I'm a failure.

Blaming yourself:
everything goes wrong
and it's all my fault.

Blaming others:
if only people were
nicer to me, I would
be a better person.

Feelings are facts:
I feel ugly, so I
must be ugly.

Do any of these sound like your self-talk? Draw a circle around any
that you recognize.

YOU'RE STRONGER THAN YOU BELIEVE. DON'T LET YOUR FEAR OWN YOU.

Michelle Hodkin

SWITCH YOUR NEGATIVE THOUGHTS INTO POSITIVE ONES

How can you transform low self-esteem and thinking errors into more positive thoughts and beliefs about yourself? Wouldn't it be great to just wave a magic wand and be the most supremely confident, high self-esteem superstar? Sadly, that's not how it works. Building self-esteem takes time and practice. The good news is, you've already started.

Here's the secret to growing your self-esteem a little bit every day. Take a negative thought and bring it up a notch. All you need to do is scooch your thought a little bit towards positivity, like this:

I'm stupid – I'm finding this really hard

I should already be able to do this – I need more practice

I look like an idiot – I look like a beginner

I can't do this – I can try my best

I should give up – I'm going to take this one step at a time

SWITCHING MY THOUGHTS

Now it's your turn. Each time a thinking error or negative thought tries to stop you or bring you down, write it here. Can you bring it up a notch? It's OK if you get stuck and need to come back to it when you're feeling a bit better about yourself.

CIRCUIT-BREAKERS

Another way of stopping self-esteem-sapping negative thoughts in their tracks is to concentrate on your body for a few moments. Try one of these circuit-breaker exercises next time you get stuck listening to negative self-talk.

Take a really deep breath through your nose, right down into your belly. Exhale slowly through your nose. Repeat three times.

Let your arms go limp and swing them sideways and upwards, then to the other side in a semi-circle. Repeat three times.

Stretch up to the ceiling, then flop down to touch your toes. Repeat three times.

Breathe deeply and bring your attention to the centre of your chest. Feel your ribcage move up and down, and your heart rate slow as you breathe in and out. Keep going for six breaths.

YOU ARE YOUR BEST THING.

Toni Morrison

MAKE A POSITIVE AFFIRMATION POSTER

Your brain grows new pathways every time you learn something new. The more you think about that new thing, the stronger its pathway will be – that's why we revise for exams.

The same happens with thoughts – if you think the same thing day after day, that thought's pathway will be incredibly strong. Because our brains are so used to these thoughts and their strong pathways, it's a real effort to think new ones, and it takes time to remember them. That's why creating new, more positive pathways to shift your thoughts and your self-esteem is so hard.

Research shows that it takes about 66 days to form a new daily habit, so it's worth putting in the effort to change your thought patterns.

One way to remind yourself of new, more positive thoughts is to have them around where you can see them. That way, every time you walk past one, that pathway in your brain will get a little stronger.

Pick one of the affirmations on pages 40–1 and write it in the frame on the next page. Then colour and decorate it to make it personal to you. Stick it somewhere where you'll see it every day, e.g. in your room, on the fridge, or on the bathroom mirror.

ACCEPT ALL
OF THE GOOD
THAT COMES
YOUR WAY
BECAUSE YOU
DESERVE IT.

Noor Tagouri

THROW OUT YOUR NEGATIVE THOUGHTS

A fun way of dealing with negative thoughts is to literally throw them out. Write them on toilet paper and flush them away; jot them on scrap paper, screw them up and throw them in the bin; or use chalk to write them on pebbles to be thrown in the sea.

Symbolically getting rid of thoughts and beliefs that you no longer want can be a powerful way to shift your thinking. The theory goes that creating something outside of yourself that represents these thoughts helps your mind to release them.

BREAK IT DOWN

Some things can seem complicated or even impossible to achieve. Low self-esteem will try to convince you not to even try something hard or time-consuming, like learning a new language or tidying a super-messy bedroom.

But with most things, once you break them down into smaller goals, you'll find that they're actually made of lots of achievable steps in the right direction that all build together toward a bigger goal.

Take skateboarding. You don't start off by learning tricks, or even moving very far. The first step in learning to skateboard is to learn how to stand still on the board, notice how it feels under your feet and find your balance. Only once you've mastered this can you begin moving, and it will take many tries to learn each small skill. But before long, with dedication, the things you found hard in the beginning will feel easy, and each skill you learn will build on the last and create new goals to aim for.

YOU ARE POWERFUL AND YOUR VOICE MATTERS.

Kamala Harris

KEEPING TRACK OF YOUR MOOD

Keeping track of your mood is a great way to become familiar with your emotions. It helps you to notice patterns and identify what affects your feelings and state of mind. Give each emotion a colour, and colour in a square for each day of the year.

If you've started your period, it's a great idea to keep track of your cycle, too, as it can have a big effect on your emotions. Try a menstrual tracker app or make a note of the first day of your period on your calendar each month.

Key: **Emotion:**

☐   ....

☐   ....

☐   ....

☐   ....

☐   ....

☐   ....

☐   ....

	J	F	M	A	M	J	J	A	S	O	N	D
1												
2												
3												
4												
5												
6												
7												
8												
9												
10												
11												
12												
13												
14												
15												
16												
17												
18												
19												
20												
21												
22												
23												
24												
25												
26												
27												
28												
29												
30												
31												

PART 4:

HOW SELF-ESTEEM CAN AFFECT YOUR ACTIONS

MAKING POSITIVE CHANGES

We've learned that negative self-talk and thinking errors make us feel bad about ourselves. These feelings can be really hard to deal with, so sometimes we act in ways that make us feel safe for a little while, but actually hurt our self-esteem in the long run.

In this section we're going to focus on these behaviours: how to spot them, why they're not helpful to you and how to change for the better.

LOW SELF-ESTEEM BEHAVIOURS

Avoidance: avoiding or choosing not to do something just because it challenges you.

Rose would love to go to football club but she's worried the other children will laugh at her while she's learning how to play, so she chooses not to go at all.

Hiding: keeping the things that make us different a secret from others.

Yusuf likes reading and writing poetry. He thinks his friends would laugh if they found out, so he keeps his hobby a secret.

Perfectionism: trying to be perfect at everything you do.

Alex has no time to relax at the weekends because she spends all her spare time revising for her upcoming exams. She thinks she'll fail at school, and her family and friends will turn their backs on her if she gets less than 100 per cent.

Passive: trying to please other people all the time, and not feeling able to say "no" to things you don't want to do.

Farah lets her friends take food from her lunch because she thinks it will make her more popular, even though it means she will feel hungry all afternoon.

Aggressive: treating others in a bossy, threatening or unkind way to make them feel bad about themselves.

Ben laughs loudly when his classmates make mistakes. When he makes a mistake, he gets really angry and storms out of the classroom.

Attention-seeking: trying to get other people to tell you that you're a good or interesting person; trying to make people feel sorry for you; doing risky or shocking things so people take notice of you.

Emmie tells lies about herself and her family because she thinks this will make her more popular. She pretends that her family live in a mansion and that she has a much older boyfriend.

Do you recognize yourself in any of these behaviours? It's OK if you do. It's very normal to act like this. Doing these things makes us feel better for a little while, but actually hurts our self-esteem in the long run.

This is because, in order to make new more positive pathways, your mind needs to have positive experiences of you being yourself. It's about teaching your brain that even if you make a mistake or stand up for yourself or do something embarrassing, your friends and family will still be there for you, and you can cope with the difficult feelings that might arise. If you don't practise being yourself, your mind won't get a chance to make new neural pathways, and that's how behaviours like the ones on the last couple of pages simply strengthen low self-esteem pathways.

Can you think of a time when low self-esteem
affected the way you acted? What happened?

If you had a time machine, and could go back and live
that moment again, would you do anything differently?

HOW TO MAKE CHANGES

The key to stopping low self-esteem affecting how you behave is learning to press pause on yourself. Low self-esteem behaviours usually happen when you're feeling a big, uncomfortable emotion... which makes it extra difficult to stop yourself from doing them!

Pressing pause on yourself means recognizing that you're feeling something huge, taking a deep breath and just staying with the feeling. You can use mindfulness here, which you learned about in Part 2.

How to press pause:

★ **Pause: stop what you're doing.**

★ **Take a deep breath.**

★ **Say to yourself (out loud, in your head or written down): "I'm feeling _____."**

★ **Notice how that emotion feels in your body.**

★ **If you feel the urge to do one of the low self-esteem behaviours, you could say, think or write: "I really want to _____."**

★ **Take three more deep breaths.**

Here's an example:

Amelie's friend Jo makes fun of her height. She calls her names and steals her pencil case, holding it higher than she can reach. Once Amelie gets her pencil case back, Jo says: "It's just a joke, Amelie, you don't mind."

Amelie presses pause. She takes a deep breath and thinks to herself, "I'm feeling humiliated and scared of losing this friendship. My throat feels tight and my face feels hot. I really want to laugh along and pretend I'm OK with what just happened." She takes three more deep breaths and says: "No, that really upset me."

Her friend is surprised. "I thought you didn't mind! Usually, you think it's funny, too."

"I was pretending before," Amelie says. "I don't like being treated in that way."

"I'm really sorry," Jo says. "I won't do it again."

After that, Jo treats Amelie with more respect and their friendship is more fun for both of them.

BE ASSERTIVE

Choosing not to let low self-esteem affect how you act takes a lot of courage. It can feel uncomfortable and even scary to admit to mistakes or stand up for yourself.

Assertiveness means speaking and acting with respect for both yourself and others. You need to behave assertively in order to create those new, high self-esteem brain pathways.

Assertive
Adjective

Being able to stand up for yourself and others in a calm, positive way.

★ Assertiveness means being truthful about what you like and dislike, rather than trying to please other people.

★ Assertiveness means being honest about your feelings, rather than expecting others to read your mind.

★ Assertiveness means saying sorry when you have hurt someone, rather than blaming them or saying it never happened.

★ Assertiveness means trying again after making a mistake, rather than giving up.

YOU GOTTA STOP WEARING YOUR WISHBONE WHERE YOUR BACKBONE OUGHTTA BE.

Elizabeth Gilbert

ASSERTIVENESS ACTION PLAN

Can you think of a habit you have that comes from low self-esteem? Perhaps the one you wrote about on page 82 – or maybe there's something you really want to stand up for yourself about, but you haven't found the courage yet.

Think about how you could use assertiveness in this situation and write about it here – you could even put together a script for yourself:

PRACTISE ASSERTIVENESS

You can use your body to practise being assertive. Research shows that rehearsing assertive movements helps you to tune into your inner strength in moments of panic or shutdown. Just as you did with positive thoughts, the more you practise speaking and moving your body in a strong, assertive way, the more natural it will feel and the easier it will be to act in this way when you need to stand up for yourself.

You'll need someone to do this exercise with, like a friend, sibling, parent or carer.

1   **Stand face to face with each other and bring both hands up to touch palms.**

2   **Think about a situation when you want to act assertively. Imagine what you will say.**

3   **Say it out loud and push the other person's hands. They should stand firm and gently resist your pushing.**

PART 5:

TAKING GOOD CARE OF YOURSELF

THE IMPORTANCE OF SELF-CARE

As you grow more independent, taking care of your emotional life becomes more important, too. Self-care's not really just about pampering baths and regular haircuts (no matter what the beauty industry might have you believe)... It's also about awareness of your physical, mental and emotional well-being, and how to take care of your whole self.

Low self-esteem can sometimes make self-care difficult. You might even feel like you don't deserve things such as enough sleep, healthy food and a good social life.

Taking care of yourself even when it's hard is an important part of building self-esteem. The better you get at noticing when you need to pay more attention to yourself, the calmer and more confident you'll be.

TAKE TIME FOR YOU

Spending time in your own company is really important for healthy self-esteem. It gives you the chance to get to know yourself and not worry about pleasing anyone else.

What do you like to do alone? Add your own!

Reading
Errands
Walking
Running
Journaling
Gaming
Painting

RELAXATION TOOLS

If you have trouble relaxing, try one of the ideas on the following pages.

BREATHING TRACK

Trace your finger slowly along the sides of this triangle. Breathe in for the first side, hold your breath for the second and breathe out for the third. See how slowly you can go.

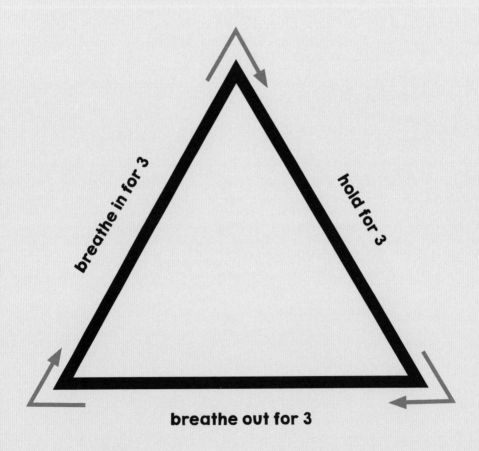

breathe in for 3

hold for 3

breathe out for 3

MAKE YOUR OWN STRESS-RELIEVER BALL

You will need:
A balloon
A small, empty plastic bottle
10 tbsp flour
Paper

Method:
Curl your paper into a funnel and use it to put the flour into the plastic bottle.

Blow up your balloon and pinch it closed with one hand. With the other, stretch the lip of the balloon over the bottle's spout, without letting the air out.

Turn the bottle upside-down and shake the flour into the balloon. Carefully remove the balloon, gently let all the air out and tie a knot to secure it.

Your relaxation ball will feel good to squeeze any time, especially when you're feeling anxious or stressed.

Balloons will break down over the course of 1–6 months, depending on how much you use your relaxation ball, so don't leave it where the flour could cause a mess. You can strengthen it with a second balloon to help it last longer.

YOGA STRETCHES

Yoga is beneficial for mental health because it focuses the mind, slows down your breathing and releases stress. The mindful, non-competitive nature of yoga is also great for self-esteem.

Starting your day with some simple yoga stretches will help you feel more awake and positive first thing in the morning. If you practise regularly, you'll gradually feel your muscles become more flexible and the stretches become easier, bringing a sense of accomplishment.

Here's a morning yoga routine to try:

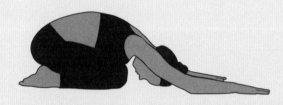

Child's pose: kneel on the floor with your toes together and your knees hip-width apart. Lower your forehead to the floor and stretch your arms forward. Hold for three breaths.

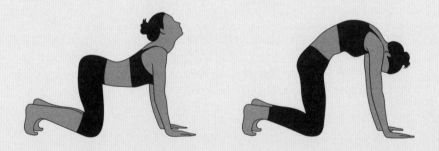

Cat-cow stretch: begin on your hands and knees with a flat spine. Inhale to lift your head, relax your shoulders and look ahead. Exhale to lower your head, lift your spine and look at your knees. Repeat three times.

Thread the needle: begin on your hands and knees. Sit back onto your feet with your arms stretched forward. Take your right arm and slide it under your left, looking all the time at your right hand. Now repeat with the other arm.

Downward dog: begin on your hands and knees. Exhale to straighten your legs and push the floor away with your hands. Hold for three breaths.

COLOURING

Research shows that colouring is just as beneficial to our emotional and mental health as meditation. Just like meditation, it focuses the mind on the moment, allowing the brain to switch off from other thoughts.

Relax and enjoy colouring this page.

WE MIGHT HAVE TO, SOMETIMES, BE BRAVE ENOUGH TO SWITCH THE SCREENS OFF IN ORDER TO SWITCH OURSELVES BACK ON.

Matt Haig

SOCIAL MEDIA AND YOU

Social media is a huge part of how we communicate with one another, find out what's going on in the world, shop and express ourselves. It can be a really positive thing, but it can also have a massive, negative effect on mental health.

- Research by the Royal Society for Public Health found that using social media can lead to increased depression, anxiety, poor body image and loneliness in teenagers.

- Thirty-one per cent of teens say social media has a mostly positive impact on them.

Next time you use social media, check in with yourself. What sensations are you feeling in your body? What emotions are coming up? Jot them down here:

BE KIND ONLINE

The internet exists to connect, entertain and inform us. It's really important, though, to not let it overwhelm us. That means putting up a boundary – unfriending, unfollowing, muting or blocking – between you and anything online that makes you feel bad about yourself, controlled, scared or ashamed. For example, if you notice you're comparing yourself harshly with someone else online, it could be time for a break from following that person. Likewise, if you find reading the news stressful right now, it's OK to take a break.

Behind every online profile is a human being. Just like in real life, you need to treat others with respect and expect respect in return. If someone treats you in a way that's unacceptable, you can use the assertiveness skills you learned on page 88 to communicate your feelings clearly. Or, alternatively, you can simply disengage.

Make sure your feed is filled with positive, relatable content that is in keeping with your values and builds up your self-esteem.

SELF-CARE IS ALSO NOT ARGUING WITH PEOPLE WHO ARE COMMITTED TO MISUNDERSTANDING YOU.

Ayishat Akanbi

GET CREATIVE

Getting away from screens and creating something is great for self-esteem. Here's why: there's no right or wrong way of doing creative activities, so they give your brain a break from stressing about whether what you're doing is "good enough". This frees you up to simply have fun and see what happens – enjoying both the process and the thing you make.

Here are some ideas to try for creative activities:

Dance to your favourite song.

Sketch an outfit for a special occasion.

Start collecting something (like vintage postcards or seashells).

Draw an object from your bedroom.

Learn how to safely build a campfire.

Write a poem about what you see out of the window.

TREAT YOURSELF

Instead of seeing time spent alone as being a drag, set a date and time, and plan some alone time you can look forward to. Wear clothes you feel great in and pick an activity that feels like a treat.

It could be as simple as watching your favourite TV show or as fancy as baking yourself a cake.

Having fun alone is fantastic for self-esteem, and thinking of it as a date will help you to like yourself even more.

What will you do to treat yourself?

How did it go? Write about what happened and how you felt:

DON'T COMPARE
YOURSELF TO OTHERS

It's easy to see the best in our friends, but difficult to offer that same generous, patient attitude to ourselves. Why is that?

Most of the time, and especially online, we get to choose what other people see of our lives, and we only let them see the parts we're proud of. For example, if you're learning to sing, you wait until you get pretty good at it before doing it in front of an audience. On the flip side, we see *all* of our own lives – the failures, the embarrassing or boring bits and the amount of hard work that goes into just being a human.

So, whenever you compare yourself to someone else, you're comparing your whole, no-filter, messy life with a narrow, rose-tinted version of the other person's.

You might assume that your friend was born with an amazing singing voice, and that's because you didn't see all the practice and bum notes that got her there.

The simple message is:

**Don't compare your behind-the-scenes
with someone else's highlight reel.**

YOU ARE UNIQUE

Have you ever taken a close look at your eyes? Did you know that no two human irises are the same? Yes, even your two irises! Just like fingerprints, the colourful part of your eye is made up of one-of-a-kind patterns.

Grab a mirror and colouring pencils, and take a really good look at your eyes. Can you draw an eye self-portrait?

Discovering your own uniqueness goes way beyond your eyeballs! Your emotions, personality, tastes, appearance... everything about you is a totally one-off blend. Just like everybody else, you are utterly irreplaceable, complex, and worthy of respect and joy.

NO ONE IS YOU AND THAT IS YOUR BIGGEST POWER.

Dave Grohl

A DIFFERENT POINT OF VIEW

A big test of self-esteem can come when we disagree with someone. If you have low self-esteem, it's easy to assume that the other person's opinion is worth more than yours, or that it's easier or more polite to simply agree. You might be worried that you'll lose the friendship or respect of that person if you don't agree with them.

But it's always possible to respectfully disagree. Friends don't have to agree on everything... As long as they respect each other's opinions, it actually makes for a more interesting friendship!

We all have different experiences and levels of knowledge, so there's always something to learn from each other. Try asking questions, and if the conversation feels too much for you, it's OK to change the subject.

If someone is putting pressure on you to agree with them and it doesn't feel right, you don't have to explain yourself or change your mind for them. You can respectfully end the conversation any time you like.

Can you think of something you've disagreed with a friend about? What happened?

Now think of a time when you changed your mind - what caused you to do that?

It's OK to disagree, and it's OK to change your mind.

WHAT ARE YOUR VALUES?

Values are the qualities and beliefs that are important to you, no matter what. Everyone has different values, and what's important to you might not be quite as important to someone else.

For example, one person might value honesty more highly than kindness, and therefore tell their friend when an outfit looks terrible. Someone who values kindness over honesty would tell a white lie to make their terribly dressed friend feel good. Both people are acting within their own value system, being themselves and doing what they think is right.

MY VALUES

What are your values? Tick the box to indicate how important each of these are to you:

	very important	quite important	not important
Loyal			
Creative			
Honest			
Kind			
Optimistic			
Reliable			
Positive			
Realistic			
Serious			
Funny			
Disciplined			
Healthy			
In control			
Spiritual			
Helpful			
Informed			
Ethical			

Can you come up with a top three? What are the most important values you live by? Write them below.

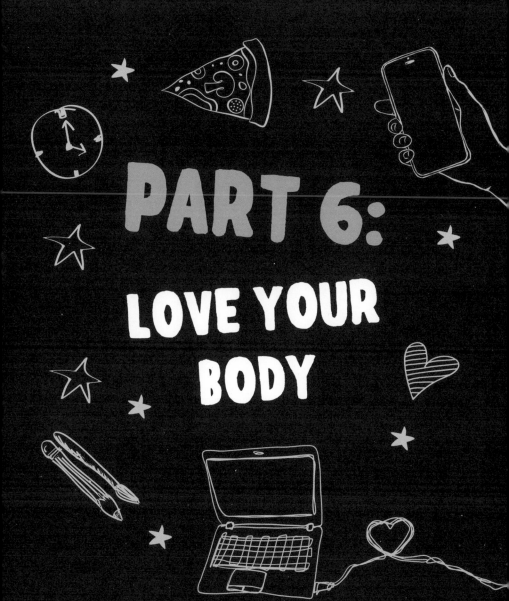

PART 6:

LOVE YOUR BODY

LOVING YOUR BODY

The way you feel about your body is closely linked to your self-esteem. That's not to say that you need to think you have a "perfect" body in order to feel good about yourself – quite the opposite!

Being comfortable with how you look and not comparing yourself to others are signs of high self-esteem. Your body is OK as it is, and so is everybody else's.

If you spend a lot of time worrying about your body and thinking it's not good enough, it can be really hard to cultivate love for it. Be gentle and patient with yourself, and remember that thoughts are just thoughts – they aren't facts.

Remember:

How your body looks is not the most important thing about you.

You do not exist for other people to look at.

Your body is just right for you.

SELF-CARE AND SELF-LOVE

It can be tricky to strike a balance between taking care of your body and changing it because you worry it's not good enough. Many of the messages we get from the beauty industry mix up the two.

A good way of finding that balance is to think about what you are aiming for. Let's say you have a skincare routine each morning. Are you looking for clean, comfortable-feeling skin... or are you aiming for perfect skin?

Clean, comfortable-feeling skin might involve a cleanser and moisturizer. Aiming for perfect skin calls for expensive products and sometimes painful scrubbing or squeezing.

We're shown images and messages about how men and women are "supposed" to look from such a young age that it can feel natural to want to change your body to fit what you see in the media. Loving yourself as you are is a brave thing to do, and many people might not understand it.

Choosing to opt out of things like removing body hair, wearing gendered clothes or putting on make-up is a personal choice available to everyone.

Remember:
perfect doesn't exist – most images online are edited and retouched or have a filter added, so don't trust what you see on the internet.

AFFIRMATIONS FOR LOVING YOUR BODY JUST AS IT IS

I CAN FEEL GOOD, REGARDLESS OF MY APPEARANCE.

MY BODY IS PRECIOUS.

MY BODY TAKES GOOD CARE OF ME.

I get to make decisions about my body.

I CAN TAKE GOOD CARE OF MY BODY.

MY BODY IS POWERFUL.

I AM OK
EXACTLY
AS I AM.

I don't want to
look like anyone
but myself.

My body
is mine.

MY WEIGHT MAY
CHANGE, MY
VALUE DOES NOT.

I ACCEPT MY
BODY AS IT IS
TODAY.

FOOD
nourishes
my body.

OTHERS' OPINIONS
OF MY BODY DO
NOT AFFECT OR
INVOLVE ME.

IN A SOCIETY THAT PROFITS FROM YOUR SELF-DOUBT, LIKING YOURSELF IS A REBELLIOUS ACT.

Caroline Caldwell

YOUR CHANGING BODY

As you grow into a young adult, your body will go through changes. You know about puberty and what to expect... but do you know how to keep your self-esteem high while you experience it?
   Here are some tips to keep in mind:

★ **If you experience touching, uncomfortable comments or inappropriate attention without your consent at any time, it's not your fault – you can report this to the police or a trusted adult. Your body is yours alone.**

★ **Everyone goes through puberty at a different rate, and it can be just as distressing to be a late developer as an early one. Be patient with yourself and remember that it's not a competition.**

★ **Stay in touch with your body by keeping active. This will help you to focus on your body in ways that have nothing to do with appearance.**

★ **Talk to older siblings, parents and relatives – they have been through puberty and will have words of wisdom to offer you.**

★ **Everyone has embarrassing moments, and they remember their own much more than other people's, just like you do.**

★ **Masturbation is normal, healthy and excellent for your self-esteem. Getting to know your own body and what feels good is a really important step in growing up.**

I LIKE MYSELF

Pick a part of your body that you like. It can be anywhere – perhaps a toenail or the tip of your nose.

Can you think of three compliments to pay this part of your body? They could be about how it looks, how it takes care of you or what it helps you to do – you decide!

SOMEONE ELSE'S BEAUTY IS NOT THE ABSENCE OF YOUR OWN.

Anonymous

HOW TO EXERCISE FOR MIND AND BODY

Everyone knows exercise is good for your physical health – that's a no-brainer. But what about your mental health?

When you exercise, your body releases chemicals called endorphins that trigger positive feelings, reducing pain, stress and anxiety while boosting energy levels. Being able to influence your mood in this way, just by doing moderate physical exercise, helps to build self-esteem, because you feel more in control of your mind, body and outlook on life.

A little bit of exercise that you enjoy doing regularly will build a healthy habit. Here are some of the best forms of exercise for self-esteem, as recommended by experts:

* **Cycling**

* **Yoga**

* **Dancing**

* **Gardening**

* **Jogging**

* **Swimming**

* **Walking**

EXERCISE PLANNER

What kind of exercise would you like to try? Maybe you already have a favourite. Can you find time for a daily activity? Just half an hour every day is enough to have a positive impact on your self-esteem.

Jot down your average week on this planner, and see where you can fit exercise in:

Monday	Tuesday	Wednesday	Thursday

Friday	Saturday	Sunday

EAT WELL

Healthy self-esteem means treating your body with respect, and that includes what you eat! Growth spurts, hormones and lifestyle can affect your appetite, so stay tuned into your body's hunger signals.

Take a moment to think mindfully about your hunger levels – where are you right now?

1   **Painfully hungry**

2   **So hungry it's affecting your mood**

3   **Hungry, in need of energy**

4   **I could eat**

5   **Neutral**

6   A bit full but not completely satisfied

7   Comfortably full

8   A bit too full

9   So full you feel sleepy

10   Painfully full

A healthy diet is made up of a wide variety of foods – carbs, protein, fat, fruit and veg, sugar, and plenty of water. Go for a good balance of three meals with healthy snacks in between, and try not to let yourself get uncomfortably hungry or full.

SLEEP TIGHT

The more well-rested you are, the better you'll feel about yourself. Research shows that optimism and high self-esteem are closely linked to having a good night's sleep. We've all felt grouchy after a late night from time to time, and being tired increases feelings of anxiety and low mood.

Teens' body clocks are different to those of children and adults. You naturally fall asleep and wake up later as a teenager, so it can be tricky to make sure you're getting enough sleep, while also keeping up with school and the rest of your family.

Checking in with your body will help you to establish a good sleep routine – it will tell you when it's time to rest. Space school projects out so you don't find yourself pulling an all-nighter. Put down your phone or book at the same time every night and make sure your bedroom is a calm, pleasant place to be.

NIGHT-TIME ROUTINE

Having a regular routine before you go to bed will help you relax and fall asleep more quickly. Doing the same thing every evening helps signal to your body and mind that it's time to switch off and rest.

Have a think about what could make up your night-time routine. Here are some ideas to get you started:

- ★ **A warm bath**
- ★ **A cup of camomile tea**
- ★ **A glass of milk**
- ★ **A spritz of lavender pillow-spray**
- ★ **A chapter of a book**
- ★ **Burning an incense stick**
- ★ **A hot shower**
- ★ **Listening to a guided meditation**
- ★ **Turning down the lights**
- ★ **Texting goodnight to your bestie**

My night-time routine

.... Time: ....

.... Time: ....

.... Time: ....

.... Time: ....

.... Time: ....

.... Time: ....

PART 7:

YOUR PLACE IN THE WORLD

FIND WHAT INSPIRES YOU

As your self-esteem grows, you'll feel increasingly free to be yourself and follow your gut.

It might feel like you need to make big decisions about your life over the next few years, but remember that you are allowed to change your mind – it's OK to see where life takes you and make choices one at a time.

Work hard, stand up for yourself and if a situation doesn't feel right to you, it's OK to ask questions or to leave. It's OK to decide that something isn't for you, and it's OK to try something completely new.

You will grow into a hundred different versions of yourself as you go through life. It's OK to be who you are today.

EXPECTATIONS

It may feel like a lot is expected of you while you're a teen, and that can be a lot of pressure.

What expectations or pressures do you feel from parents, school, the media or other sources? Write about them here:

Some of those expectations will be helpful ones – like the expectation that you try your best at school – and will help to motivate you to fulfil your potential. Others will be unhelpful – like pressures around how you look – and will make you feel like you're not good enough.

Which expectations are helpful to you?

Which expectations are unhelpful to you?
What would it feel like to let go of them?

Can you use an affirmation from this book, or one that you've made up, to help you think about one of these expectations differently? For example, if you feel pressure to be a perfect student, you might say to yourself: "I deserve to relax" or "I am doing enough".

While we cannot control other people or the outside world, we can influence how we think and feel about the things we experience.

YOUR FRIENDSHIP CIRCLE

Friendships are really important to your self-esteem. Over the next couple of pages there are a few questions to help you think about and reflect on your friendships.

Who is in your circle of friends? Write their names here. Can you think of one word to describe each friend?

What qualities make a good friend?

If one of your friends hurt your feelings, would you feel able to tell them? Why?

In what ways are you similar to your friends?

In what ways are you different from your friends?

How do you feel when you're with friends?

JUST DO THE NEXT RIGHT THING, ONE THING AT A TIME.

Glennon Doyle

FRIENDSHIPS AND RELATIONSHIPS

As you mature, your friendships will naturally become more and more important to you. If you want to, you might develop romantic relationships, too. You're still very much an important part of your family, but with growing independence, you'll want to be able to choose who you spend your free time with.

If you struggle with low self-esteem, it can be easy to end up in bad friendships with people who make you feel that you can't be yourself around them. This isn't your fault. As you begin to stand up for yourself, you may find that some people don't like it. As you grow and change, it's OK for your friendships to change, too, and it's much better to be alone than hang out with someone who makes you feel bad about yourself. Treat yourself and everyone you meet with the respect you want to be shown, and you'll find that your relationships with others get better and better.

WHAT MAKES A GOOD FRIEND OR RELATIONSHIP? AND WHAT MAKES A BAD ONE?

Whether it's a romantic relationship or you're just friends, there are certain things to look for in a person that will help you work out if they're a good fit for you.

Positive	Negative
Lets you be yourself	Puts you down for who you are
Lets you choose your friends	Controls who you see
Replies to your messages	Ignores or ghosts you
Is considerate of your feelings	Treats you like your feelings don't matter
Is interested in your thoughts, feelings and experiences	Is not interested in what you have to say
Makes you feel safe	Makes you feel anxious or unsafe
Laughs with you	Laughs at you
You can tell them if they've upset you	Refuses to acknowledge that they've upset you
They want to hang out with you	They will drop you for other plans

WHAT TO DO IF YOU ARE IN A BAD FRIENDSHIP OR RELATIONSHIP

If you're in a friendship or relationship where you feel unsafe or like you can't leave, it's not your fault. This can happen to anyone and the blame lies solely with the person who is treating you disrespectfully. They may use guilt or threats to stop you from walking away. Remember: you are not responsible for the consequences of their actions. If they treat others badly, it is natural that people will not want to be around them.

There are many people you can talk to if you're unsure about someone in your life. Think of a friend or an adult that you know and trust. Then check out page 140 for more resources. You're not alone and you deserve to be treated well.

"no" ISN'T A BAD WORD, THOUGH PEOPLE TRY TO MAKE US FEEL GUILTY FOR SETTING OUR PERSONAL BOUNDARIES.

Karamo Brown

PART 8:

LOOKING FORWARD

YOU'VE GOT THIS!

How you feel now is not how you'll always feel. Life will have its ups and downs. The key is to feel strong in yourself and trust that, whatever happens, you will cope and things will be OK.

Some days, it'll be easy to feel good about yourself – enjoy those days, you deserve them. Other days, it will be hard. You'll mess up or miss the mark, or other people will try to bring you down. This happens to everybody – if it doesn't happen to you, you're not doing life properly! Keep people around you who will remind you how brilliant, strong and special you are, especially on tough days.

Healthy self-esteem is a lifelong project, and getting into the habit of treating yourself with kindness while you're a teen will be the greatest gift you can give your future self.

YOU'RE NOT ALONE

I used to be friends with a group of girls who teased me. It made me feel embarrassed but they always said they were just joking. When I said I didn't want to hang out with them any more, I was left without many friends for a bit. It was hard, but I have friends again now, who are actually nice to me, so it was worth it.

Aisha, 13

If I see something on social media that makes me feel like I need to change my body, I just unfollow. Life's too short to compare myself to strangers on the internet – I'm fabulous exactly as I am.

Alex, 15

I've always been pretty quiet. I used to think there was something wrong with me – that I was boring and I should be more chatty, loud and silly. Recently, though, I've learned to accept that being an introvert is a wonderful part of who I am, and there's nothing wrong with it.

Jack, 14

I've always had crushes on girls rather than boys. I kept it a secret and tried to fancy boys, but I just couldn't. Last year we had a new girl join my netball squad who is a proud lesbian. We're not each other's type but it feels good to know I'm not alone, and to have a friend who feels the same as I do.

Hazel, 15

ASK FOR HELP

If you're struggling with low self-esteem, or any other aspect of mental health, there are lots of organizations out there that can provide help and advice. If you feel like your mental health is becoming more than you can manage, it's a good idea to talk with an adult you trust and make an appointment with a doctor.

Anxiety UK
03444 775 774 (helpline)
07537 416 905 (text)
www.anxietyuk.org.uk
Advice and support for
people living with anxiety.

BEAT
0808 801 0711
www.beateatingdisorders.co.uk
Under-18s helpline, webchat
and online support groups for
people with eating disorders,
such as anorexia and bulimia.

**Campaign Against Living
Miserably (CALM)**
0800 58 58 58
www.thecalmzone.net
Provides listening services,
information and support,
including a webchat, for
anyone who needs to talk.

Childline
0800 1111
www.childline.org.uk
Support for young people
in the UK, including a
free 24-hour helpline.

FRANK
0300 123 6600
www.talktofrank.com
Confidential advice and
information about drugs,
their effects and the law.

The Jed Foundation
1 800 273 8255
www.jedfoundation.org
Information and advice for US
teens to promote emotional
and mental health.

**National Alliance on
Mental Illness (NAMI)**
1 800 950 6264
www.nami.org
Information and advice
on managing mental
health for US teens.

On My Mind
020 7794 2313
www.annafreud.org/on-my-mind
Information for young
people to make informed
choices about their mental
health and well-being.

Young Minds
0808 802 5544
www.youngminds.org.uk
Information about every
aspect of mental well-
being for young people.

Refuge
0808 2000 247
www.refuge.org.uk
Advice about domestic abuse and
support for those affected by it.

FURTHER READING

Check out these books for teens about self-esteem, mental health and
being your best self:

Man Down
Charlie Hoare

Positively Teenage
Nicola Morgan

Eleanor and Park
Rainbow Rowell

The Confidence Code for Girls
Claire Shipman and Katty Kay

Just As You Are
Michelle Skeen and Kelly Skeen

Stargirl
Jerry Spinelli

You Are Awesome
Matthew Syed

Wolfpack
Abby Wambach

*The Self-Care Kit for
Stressed-Out Teens*
Frankie Young

CONCLUSION

You are strong and capable, even when you don't feel like it. Building up your self-esteem and keeping it high takes work, and it's OK to take your time and stumble along the way. It's these stumbles that will help you grow stronger.

You've Got This! rules to live by:

Accept yourself as you are.

Know that you are capable of anything.

Reach out for support when you need it.

It takes courage to be in the world and you can trust yourself to handle whatever life throws at you. You've most definitely got this!

NEVER LET SOMEONE STOP YOU OR SHAME YOU FOR BEING YOURSELF.

Lizzo

If you're interested in finding out more about our
books, find us on Facebook at Summersdale Publishers,
on Twitter at @Summersdale and on
Instagram at @summersdalebooks.

www.summersdale.com

IMAGE CREDITS